# The Nutty Nut Chase

To our little Anthony,
from Mommy + Daddy
Oct. 6, 2005

For David, with love
~KW

For Cassie
~VC

ISBN 0-439-82404-4

Copyright © 2004 by Good Books, Intercourse, PA 17534.
Text copyright © 2004 by Kathryn White.
Illustrations copyright © 2004 by Vanessa Cabban.
All rights reserved. Published by Scholastic Inc., 557 Broadway, New York, NY 10012,
by arrangement with Good Books. SCHOLASTIC and associated logos are
trademarks and/or registered trademarks of Scholastic Inc.

12 11 10 9 8 7 6 5 4 3 2                    5 6 7 8 9 10/0

Printed in the U.S.A.                                    40

First Scholastic printing, October 2005

# The Nutty Nut Chase

Kathryn White    *Illustrated by* Vanessa Cabban

SCHOLASTIC INC.

New York  Toronto  London  Auckland  Sydney
Mexico City  New Delhi  Hong Kong  Buenos Aires

Hickory was making rude faces at Pecan
when the strangest thing happened.

POP!

A shiny brown nut suddenly burst up from the ground. It wobbled and shook, wibbled and quivered, then lay there, teasingly delicious.

"Wow, lunch!" Pecan shouted.

"Wow, lunch and dinner!" Hickory screeched.

"It's my nut," said Pecan.

"It's mine," snapped Hickory.

"Who's making that noise?" shouted Badger.
"I'm trying to sleep."
All the animals came out to see what was happening.

"My nut!" Pecan shouted.

"It's mine!" yelled Hickory. "I saw it first."

"Did not."

"Did so."

"Bop his nose!" shouted Littlest Rabbit.

"Certainly not. Bopping noses doesn't solve problems," said Badger firmly.

"There will be a competition and the winner will get the nut."

"I know," said Hedgehog. "The prickliest wins the nut."
"But you're the prickliest," said Pecan and Hickory.
"So I am!" said Hedgehog, delighted. "I win! I get the nut."
"Cuddliest gets the nut," said Littlest Rabbit, "I win!"

# "Enough!"

said Badger. "We will have a
race. First to reach the post wins."
"Hooray, a race!" everyone cheered.

Blackbird whistled the
start of the race. They were off.
Pecan and Hickory shot ahead
but the rabbits were close behind.
Hedgehog tried to run but only managed
a waddle. In a huff, he curled himself into
a ball and rolled full speed down the slope.
    Littlest Rabbit looked back to see a prickly
ball spinning towards them. "Look out!"
he called. Too late!

Hedgehog crashed through
the racers like a cannonball
and everyone landed in a
prickly heap.
  "Oh dear," tutted Badger.
"We'll have to start again.
And prickly cannonballs
aren't allowed."

Hedgehog snorted and sulked off.

Blackbird whistled and they were off again.
Pecan and Hickory were neck and neck.
"My nut!" shouted Pecan triumphantly. "I win!"
"No!" shouted Hickory. "It's mine! I win!"

Suddenly the nut began to move. It twitched
and jerked, joggled and jiggled until PLOP!
It disappeared down under the ground.
  "It's a magic nut!" shouted Littlest Rabbit.
  "Nutty magic!" squealed Hedgehog, racing back to see.
  "Bet it would have tasted magic too," said Shrew.

POP!
The nut sprang up
right in front of Shrew.
  "Quick, grab it!" shouted Littlest Rabbit.
  All the animals shot across the grass, rolling and shrieking,
    jumping and hopping, banging and bopping into each other.
  "I've got it!" shouted Hedgehog, but the nut vanished again.
  "That's my nose!" Shrew squeaked.

"Shhhhh!" said Badger suddenly. "Look."

He pointed at the magic nut that had appeared at his feet. Everyone tiptoed up to it. The nut shook and quivered. The animals looked in amazement.

"Help!" squealed the nut.

"AAAH!" shrieked Littlest Rabbit. "A talking nut."

"You're a talking nut," said Pecan.

Pecan and Hickory bent down and pulled and tugged, yanked and wrenched at the nutshell with all their might.

# POP!

Out flew the nutshell, sending Pecan and Hickory rolling backwards. And there, where the nut had been, was Mole!

Mole shook himself and stood up on his two tiny legs. "Thanks!" he said. "I thought I would be stuck in that nutshell forever."

Littlest Rabbit put the empty shell on his head. "It makes a great hat," he giggled.

"That looked like the tastiest nut ever," groaned Pecan and Hickory.

"There's plenty more where that came from," chirped Mole and he disappeared underground.

Suddenly shiny nuts began
popping up all over the place.
   "There's enough for everyone,"
Mole chuckled.

POP!  POP!